This igloo book belongs to:

D0246202

....

igloobooks

Published in 2016
by Igloo Books Ltd, Cottage Farm, Sywell, NN6 0BJ
www.igloobooks.com

Illustrated by Spike Maguire
Written by Emily Johnson

Designed by Kerri-Ann Hulme
Edited by Stephanie Moss

LEO002 0216
2 4 6 8 10 9 7 5 3 1
ISBN 978-1-78440-422-2

Printed and manufactured in China

What About Me?

igloobooks

When I was staying at Grandma's house, the doorbell rang at three.

"Hello, Benji," said my parents, walking in and hugging me.

They had something in a blanket.

It was **gurgly** and **pink**.

"Well?" said Mummy, showing me.

"What do you think?"

Daddy said, "This is Bonnie. She's your baby sister. You're her big brother," he added. Then, Dad bent down and kissed her.

"I don't want a sister!"

I cried. "When is she going back?"

Mummy and Daddy smiled and said...

... "It doesn't work like that."

After that, **strange** things
began to happen during the night.
There were footsteps in the hall
and clicking on and off of the light.

Mum and Dad were always leaning over Bonnie's cot. They made soft sighing sounds and **cooed and ooed** a lot.

It was Bonnie **this** and Bonnie **that**.

Nobody noticed me at all.

I felt like I was
invisible...

... even when I did **cartwheels** down the hall.

Night after night I lay awake, thinking in my bed.

Then suddenly, a **plan** began to form inside my head.

I'd **make** Mum and Dad notice me.

I'd amuse··· ···delight··· ···transfix·

But no one seemed to notice my special magic tricks.

I tried juggling and singing...

... even ballet dancing, too.

All that Mummy said, was,
"What's got into you?"

After another night of...

...screaming,

I pulled open my closet door.

I dragged out the dressing-up box and flung **everything** onto the floor.

I put on my red mask and my **superhero** cape.

Then I dived into the hallway to make a **daring** escape.

I raced along the carpet...

... but **tripped** over the cat.

MEOW!
YOWL!

... he went as he **hissed** and **spat**.

"What's that?"

... called Dad, from behind the bedroom door.

Very carefully, **I slunk** away along the hallway floor.

Down the stairs, one by one,
like a superhero I crept.

I almost
made it
to the bottom...

... when suddenly,
I stepped...

I hurried back upstairs,
quick march, at the double.
I knew that the next day...

... I'd **really** be
in trouble.

I didn't want to get up
when next morning came.

Then, from downstairs, my **dad** called my name.

I was sure Mum and Dad would be angry, but they were smiling instead.

"Don't worry, Benji, we know you've been feeling left out," they said.

They were throwing a party that was **all about me.**

After all, I was a very important part of our **family!**

A gatekeeper gave them each a pair of green glasses and led them to the wizard's palace.

"I'll help you, if you help me," said the wizard.

"First, you must kill the wicked witch!"

The wicked witch lived in a castle guarded by wolves and crows.

Grrrrr

But the tinman fought
off the wolves.

And the scarecrow scared away the crows.

Furious, the witch summoned her flying monkeys.
Soon the friends were prisoners in her castle.

"Now you're my slaves," she cackled.

"Get to work!"

Then the witch noticed Dorothy's beautiful silver shoes.

"I want those shoes," thought the witch.

She waited until
Dorothy was fetching
a pail of water...

...then she
pushed her
and pounced.

Dorothy was so annoyed, she threw the water all over the witch.

At once, the witch
melted away into
a puddle.

"She's gone!" cried Dorothy,
quickly putting on her shoes.
"We can claim our rewards."

The wizard's rewards were rather strange.

First, he gave
the scarecrow a
handful of pins.

"Now I'm as sharp as a pin."

Then he gave
the tinman a
heart-shaped
cushion.

And for the lion, there was
a bottle marked Courage.

Last of all, the wizard showed
Dorothy a hot-air balloon.
"We'll fly home!" he said.

But the ropes snapped and the balloon took off without her.
"Go to the good witch Glinda!" called the wizard. "She'll help you."

Dorothy was in despair, but her friends took her to Glinda's palace.

"I'm stuck in Oz!" Dorothy sobbed,

standing before the throne.

"Don't worry," said Glinda, kindly.
"The silver shoes will take you home."
"Just knock the heels together and wish."

Dorothy and Toto whirled through the air... and landed back on the farm.
There stood Aunt Em, in front of a brand-new farmhouse.

Dorothy ran up and threw her arms around her. "I've been on an
amazing adventure," she said. "But oh! I'm so glad to be home."

And Toto barked as if to say, "Me too!"

Edited by Jenny Tyler and Lesley Sims
Designed by Louise Flutter, Laura Wood and Emily Bornoff
Digital design: John Russell